"With Hope
    We Can All Find Ogo Pogo"

   – written by . . . Brock Tully
   – illustrations by . . . Soren Henrich
   – edited by . . . Sherry Merk, Dianne Prytula,
          & Laurie Stapelton.

Other books by Brock Tully . . .
  1. "Coming Together" — a 10,000 mile bicycle
                        journey.
  2. "Reflections — for someone special"

*Ogo Pogo is a legendary monster who many people claim they have sighted in Lake Okanagan, British Columbia, Canada.

– printed on recycled paper

INTRODUCTION

Up to 1970 i probably appeared happy enough, but for me it wasn't enough and inside i wasn't happy. i wasn't feeling good about the way i was living, but i was living the way i thought i was supposed to. i actually felt i had landed on this planet by some mistake!

In 1970 i hopped on my bicycle and travelled 10,000 miles, through Canada, the United States, and Mexico. What began as a physical challenge soon became "much more;" i was getting to know myself and i was becoming closer to my heart. i appropriately named my first book "Coming Together."

My journey has since become one of taking risks and facing challenges, following my heart, and going after my dreams.

With Hope We Can All Find Ogo Pogo is a story about me, and i hope about you too! My bicycle trip was like the butterfly in this book and i am seeing more and more that we can all find *Ogo Pogo!*

Dedicated to . . . a peaceful world.

Inspired by . . .
   those who believe
                  that peace begins
         when we have
                        peace within.

   i have been strongly influenced and touched by Gandhi, Martin Luther King, Leo Buscaglia ("Living, Loving, and Learning"), Hermann Hesse ("Sidhartha"), Antoine de Saint Exupery ("The Little Prince"), Richard Bach ("Jonathan Livingston Seagull"), A.A. Milne ("Winnie-the-Pooh"), and Jerry Jampolsky ("Love Is Letting Go of Fear") . . .

      . . . to name only a few!

Early one summer evening, as the sun waved good-bye to everyone and everything after enjoying a full day of sharing its warmth and love, a small, glowing flying saucer came zooming in and out of the trees and gently landed in a soft patch of long grass and wildflowers near Lake Okanagan on the planet "Irth." Irth was a place of many strange happenings caused mainly by a confusing, but powerful creature, called "Peepels."

Within moments, the door of the saucer opened and out popped a chubby, cuddly, fuzzy little ball of fluff with a big, warm and excited smile. He was neither a Peepel nor "Animole," but rather a combination of both. He was surrounded with a warm, loving glow. His name was "Hope."

Hope couldn't believe his eyes!! There were plants and trees and flowers, and little animoles flying and running around. He loved how a soft wind, a peaceful silence and a lovely smell filled the air. The colors in the sky and on the ripples of the lake from the warm, smiling sun were breath-taking!! Hope's first glimpse of Irth was so overpowering . . . his first words flowed out uncontrollably . . .

. . . *"Wow, What a Beautiful Place!!"*

Hope began exploring Irth.

He sniffed and watched and listened and touched . . .

. . . danced and jumped and rolled and stood on his head and giggled with delight!!

"BOUNCE"

Hope wasn't even aware that he was being watched by a family of peepels and their big hairy dog, "Willie-dog."

The whole family instantly fell in love with Hope and invited him to their home.

The family took Hope by his fuzzy little hands and excitedly danced down the path toward their home.

Time passed.

Hope was beginning to understand pee-pels, who so often claimed to be the most intelligent of all creatures living on Irth. Pee-pels were very confusing and Hope spent much of his day in thought, trying to understand them.

. . . why is it that peepels love cuddling baby-peepels and animoles (even ones they've just met!), and yet they seem to be uncomfortable touching each other in a gentle and affectionate way?

. . . and child peepels are constantly being warned about strangers, yet they seem most often hurt by peepels they know.

Hope spent hours curled up with a good book in front of a warm, cozy fire, cuddling with Willie-dog. Mostly, however, he watched the peepels.

. . . if child-peepels are so happy just "being,"
why do grown-up peepels become so worried
about what they're "going to be?"

The family seemed so negative and untrusting of other peepels and would often sit around gossiping—yet, they were so loving to Hope and Willie-dog.

. . . if peepels love that flowers and dogs are all different colors, sizes, and kinds, why is it that those very same qualities too often separate peepels from each other?

Hope was seldom allowed out on his own, so he spent hours staring out a window watching the peepels pass by.

. . . if peepels spend so long to look their best, why is it that, when someone smiles at them and says hello, they will often give them an unfriendly look?

A beautiful butterfly often visited Hope at his bedroom window, and soon Hope and "Butty" became very good pals. Butty was always trying to encourage Hope to come outside, but Hope had too many problems about peepels to sort out, so he didn't give Butty's invitations much thought.

. . . why is it that peepels can see each other over and over again in their home town and never say hi, and yet if they see each other in another town they greet them as if they were a long lost friend?

. . . when peepels' bodies are so miraculously intricate and delicate, why are they so often disconcerned with what they eat? And when they do get sick, the pain is the last thing that happens—but the first thing they deal with.

The family of peepels spent so much of their time in the living room in front of a noisy box full of violence and pained faces. Very seldom did it show the gentleness and caring that the peepels gave to Hope and Willie-dog.

. . . peepels seem to love watching violence on TV, but are punished when they themselves are violent. Why is it that peepels who won't go to war are punished and even called "cowards" and those who kill the most, are "heroes"?

. . . why is it that child-peepels start school so excited about learning, and seem to finish so afraid of failing?

Other peepels came over to visit and the conversation was often very negative and destructive.

. . . why is it so necessary for peepels to insist that others smile for photographs? Why do so many peepels find it necessary to hide when they're feeling sad or low?

Grown-up peepels often drank alcohol. When they got really loud and out of control, Hope and Willie-dog would go to Hope's room. Butty was always there waiting and she always had an understanding look on her face.

. . . if peepels want fame and recognition so badly, why do the famous so often have long, dark-windowed cars, houses with big fences, and dogs they've trained to be mean? They seem so lonely and even though they're supposedly <u>well known</u>, no one seems to care to really know them.

Whenever the little peepels were being yelled at to settle down and be quiet, Hope would cover his ears and shudder. Tears always streamed down his chubby little cheeks.

. . . why would so many peepels care so little about the needless killing of countless whales, yet show so much caring toward two whales trapped in the ice of the arctic? . . . and why are they so scared of Russian peepels and even spend so much on weapons that can hurt them, and yet when an earthquake kills 25,000 of them, peepels send food and clothing that can help them?

Whenever Hope peeked out his door and saw the child peepels sitting silently, so full of fear, he would quietly cry to himself.

. . . i wonder how the crippled and blind feel when peepels get so drunk they can hardly walk or see.

Hope spent much of the following weeks in thought.

... why do peepels say they're "quitting" if they stop doing something they don't like? Isn't quitting staying at something they don't like, and not going after their dreams?

... why do peepels feel guilty leaving someone they _say_ they love but who they aren't very loving to? Why don't they feel guilty staying instead?

Hope was now so totally confused. His glow was gone and he had lost touch with his heart which, not long ago, was so excited about being on the planet Irth.

. . . it seems that many confused peepels are paying other peepels to unconfuse them, as they were before they "grew up."

One cloudy day, Hope felt really low and depressed. His friend Butty landed right on the window sill and waved her wing for Hope to come outside.

Hope finally decided to take a big risk and follow his inner feelings—to follow Butty. With Butty and Willie-dog's help, they lowered Hope to the ground on a few bedsheets tied securely together.

As Hope danced down the path following Butty toward Lake Okanagan, a small smile slowly crept onto his face and the glow began to reappear around him. He began to *feel* again.

Suddenly, without warning, it became very windy and began to rain. Hope stopped quickly and started to turn towards home. For the first time Butty spoke.

"What's the matter?" she asked Hope.
"It's rainy and miserable," replied Hope.

"And what's wrong with the wind and the rain?" inquired Butty.
"Look at me!" snapped Hope. "I'm all messy and soaked!"
"What do you see around you?" persisted Butty.
"Wet trees and plants blowing around like crazy!" Hope was obviously bothered by Butty's persistence.
"Look even closer!" insisted Butty.

Hope stood silent for what seemed like hours. His frown slowly changed to a tiny smile that grew . . .

and grew . . .

until his face was almost invisible behind his huge grin . . .

and he burst out . . .

"I see!! I see!!"

For the first time in quite a while, Hope began looking at things positively through the eyes of his heart, instead of negatively through the eyes of his head—that can be, so often, full of fears.

He saw the smiles of the plants as they were nourished and the glint in the eyes of the leaves as they played and frolicked in the wind. He saw the sparkle in the teeth of the trees as their huge branches hung over Hope ready to shelter or hug him. Hope even saw little elves and other animoles of the forest dancing and singing, waving and welcoming Hope into their homes of nature.

Hope continued following Butty towards the lake. His beautiful glow had fully returned!

Just as they reached a secluded little cove near the edge of the lake, Butty flew off, waving good-bye to Hope.

As Hope explored the cove with the same excitement he had when he first saw planet Irth, huge waves came lapping onto the shore.

Hope was at first startled, but as he looked out into the lake he saw two of the biggest, warmest, most loving eyes he had ever seen and he felt reassured. He was further soothed when the monster, belonging to the eyes, spoke so gently and softly, and welcomed Hope to the cove.

"Who are you?" asked Hope.
"I'm Ogo Pogo," answered Ogy.

This was the beginning of what would become a very beautiful, warm, and loving friendship.

Ogy was the most loving, forgiving, and patient living creature.

Ogy was *love!*

Ogy took Hope for rides around the cove and introduced him to many new friends. It wasn't long before Ogy shared a most wonderful secret, which really wasn't a secret at all. It was only a secret if others didn't accept Ogy (*love*) into their hearts.

Ogy could grow or shrink to any size possible, and he could even change forms!!

Hope was ecstatic at his newest realization . . .

. . . "Butty *is* Ogy . . .

. . . Ogy is in Willie-dog . . .

. . . Ogy is even in
Peepels!

. . . Hope was growing more and more toward his heart full of love and away from his head full of fears . . .

Ogy would change forms, take Hope along, and together they would spend time with some of the forest and water animoles. Everyone welcomed Ogy without fear. They were overjoyed to show Ogy and Hope how they lived. The more the animoles shared their happiness with others, the happier they became.

. . . the one thing Hope particularly noticed was how the animoles he met communicated through their love. They always worked together and considered each others' feelings. Their goal was to care and to love. Success, to them, was reaching this goal. It wasn't based on how much they made, what job they did, or what they owned. He also noticed how they handled obstacles in their lives—they weren't problems to be avoided or "numbed," but challenging opportunities to overcome . . .

The amimoles played and laughed and shared together, regardless of age, size, or color.

. . . their desire to love seemed so much
stronger than their need to be right . . .

As the animoles went about their daily chores of living, made so meaningful and enjoyable through their love, Hope saw so many similarities with the peepels.

. . . it took Hope's thoughts back to the family of peepels, who so often claimed that they were the most intelligent of all Irth's creatures. Even though they did hurt each other and step on each other to reach a goal (success), they still hung beautiful posters of love on their walls. They, too, believed in loving and sharing . . .

Hope was excited! Things were becoming clear!

. . . Hope now knew that peepels were so
full of energy and wanted so much to love, but
their fears stopped them from reaching out and
giving.

Hope <u>had been</u> a follower of the fears in his
head.

He was beginning to believe in himself and
he was becoming stronger.

He began watching less and started to join in and share with the different ani-moles Ogy introduced him to.

. . . Hope was no longer seeing others as "them" and "us,"
         but everyone as one . . .

   and every<u>thing</u>!

Hope began doing flips and somer-saults—

he was soooooo happy!!

BOING!   BOING!   BOING!

. . . Hope realized, with total joy, as shown so purely by Ogy's example, love is the greatest of all healers. With love, Hope could see the beauty in so many things and the potential beauty in the rest . . .

. . . Ogy had shown Hope that peepels had lost touch with their hearts. It wasn't all the "things" that they wanted that was so bad, it was that they had lost touch with the love of doing things <u>in the moment</u>. It's the journey of life that is so fulfilling and exciting! When peepels were motivated by the love of things they seemed to lose touch with their hearts . . .

. . . and with other hearts too!

Hope gave Ogy the biggest hug he could possibly give and, after waving good-bye to all his new pals, dashed off toward his peepels' home.

. . . he now knew he had a purpose and a goal. Hope was becoming strong in himself and so purely and humbly loving.

As Hope raced towards his home, he saw Willie-dog at the window, wagging his tail so fast it almost flew off!

Hope's heart overflowed with joy as the family of peepels rushed outside to greet him . . .

. . . and he burst out . . .

"WE ARE ALL OGO POGO!!"

He now realized that . . .

"We Can All Find Ogo Pogo" . . .

. . . we can find the love we all are.

Years later . . .

Do you know that individually and
together Hope and Willie-dog's love did
slowly change the family of peepels? Not
only that, but the family of peepels changed
their town. It snowballed and snowballed,
and do you know that instead of sending
threats to other countries, governments
began sending notes of love and friendship,
and exchanging and sharing ideas? They
were working together toward their com-
mon goal of love!

And do you know that the peepels of Irth
sent Hope in his flying saucer to all the
other planets to invite their creatures to
come and visit because they had something
beautiful and special that they wanted to
share?

And do you realize that all the creatures
of Irth finally realized that peepels are
intelligent?

. . . they just need a little wisdom
as well!

. . . success, to me, is staying in touch with my heart. i want to be an example of what i believe. Too often, i've become lazy and lost touch with myself and i've been very hard on myself for my inconsistencies and unloving behaviors. i want to let those people know how much i appreciate their support in forgiving and being patient with me and who have made it easier for me to forgive myself and "grow" . . .

. . . i only _hope_ i can give the same to others.

> "*. . . i'd rather be seen*
> *for who i am*
> *and be alone . . .*
> *than be accepted*
> *for someone i'm not*
> *and be lonely.*"

– Brock Tully –
(from Brock's book . . .
"Reflections — for someone special")